Translated by
Naomi Lewis

Hans Andersen

The Little Mermaid
and Other Fairy Tales

D1136821

PENGUIN BOOKS

PENGUIN BOOKS

Published by the Penguin Group
Penguin Books Ltd, 27 Wrights Lane, London w8 5tz, England
Penguin Books USA Inc., 375 Hudson Street, New York, New York 10014, USA
Penguin Books Australia Ltd, Ringwood, Victoria, Australia
Penguin Books Canada Ltd, 10 Alcorn Avenue, Toronto, Ontario, Canada m4v 3b2
Penguin Books (NZ) Ltd, 182–190 Wairau Road, Auckland 10, New Zealand
Penguin Books Ltd, Registered Offices: Harmondsworth, Middlesex, England

First published in *Hans Andersen's Fairy Tales* in Puffin Books 1981

This collection published in Penguin Books 1996
1 3 5 7 9 10 8 6 4 2

Copyright © Naomi Lewis, 1981
All rights reserved

Set in 12.5/14pt Bembo Monotype
Typeset by Datix International Limited, Bungay, Suffolk
Printed in England by Clays Ltd, St Ives plc

Except in the United States of America, this book is sold subject to the condition that it
shall not, by way of trade or otherwise, be lent, re-sold, hired out, or otherwise
circulated without the publisher's prior consent in any form of binding or cover other
than that in which it is published and without a similar condition including this
condition being imposed on the subsequent purchaser

Contents

The Little Mermaid

FAR, far out to sea the water is as blue as the petals of the loveliest cornflower, and as clear as the clearest glass; but it is deep, very deep, deeper than any anchor has ever sunk. Countless church towers would have to be placed one on top of one another to reach from the sea-bed to the surface. Down in those depths live the mer-people.

Now you must not think for a moment that there is nothing down below but bare white sand. No, indeed – the most wonderful trees and plants grow there, with stems and leaves so lithe and sensitive that they wave and sway with the slightest stir of the water; they might be living creatures. All kinds of fish, both large and small, glide in and out of the branches, just like birds in the air up here. In the very deepest part of all is the Mer-King's palace. Its walls are of coral, and the long pointed windows are of the clearest amber, while the roof is made of cockleshells, which open and close with the waves. That's a splendid sight, for each holds a shining pearl; any single one would be the pride of a queen's crown.

The Mer-King here had been a widower for many years; his dowager mother kept house for him. She was a wise old lady, though rather too proud of her royal rank; that's why she always wore twelve oysters on her tail while other high-born mer-folk were allowed no more than six. But she deserved special praise for the care she took of the little mer-princesses, her granddaughters.

There were six of them, all beautiful, but the youngest was the most beautiful of all. Her skin was like a rose petal, pure and clear; her eyes were as blue as the deepest lake. But, like the others, she had no feet; her body ended in a fish's tail. All day long she and her sisters would play down there in the palace, in and out of the vast rooms where living sea-flowers grew from the walls. When the great amber windows were open the fish would swim inside and let themselves be stroked.

2 Outside the palace was a large garden with

flame-red and sea-blue trees. The fruit all shone like gold, and the flowers looked like glowing fire among the moving stems and leaves. The ground itself was of the finest sand, but blue as a sulphur flame. A strange blue-violet light lay over everything; you might have thought that, instead of being far down under the sea, you were high up in the air, with nothing over and under you but sky. On days of perfect calm you could see the sun; it looked like a crimson flower, with rays of light streaming out of its centre.

Each of the little princesses had her own small plot in the garden, where she could dig and plant whatever she wished. One made her flower-bed in the shape of a whale; another made hers like a mermaid. But the youngest had hers perfectly round, like the sun, and the only flowers she planted there were like smaller suns in their glow and colour.

She was a strange child, quiet and thoughtful. While the other sisters decorated their gardens with wonderful things from the wrecks of ships, the only ornament she would have was a 3 beautiful marble carving, a lovely boy made out of pure white stone. This too had sunk to the sea-bed from a wreck. Beside this marble boy she planted a rose-red tree like a weeping willow; it grew apace, its branches bending over the stone figure until they touched the deep-blue sand below.

Nothing pleased the youngest princess more than to hear about the far-off world of humans. She made the old grandmother tell her all she knew about ships and towns, people and animals. It was a strange and wonderful thought to her that the flowers on earth had a sweet smell, for they had none at all in the sea.

'As soon as you are fifteen,' the grandmother told her granddaughters, 'you may rise to the surface, and sit on the rocks in the moonlight and watch the great ships sail by. If you have enough courage you may even see woods and towns!' The following year the oldest of the sisters would be fifteen; but as for the others – well, each was a year younger than the next, so the youngest of them all still had five years to wait. But each promised to tell the rest what she had seen, and what she had found most surprising in the human world above. Their grandmother never told them enough, and there was so much they wanted to know.

But none of the six had a greater wish to learn about the mysterious earth above than the youngest (the very one who had the longest time to wait), the one who was so thoughtful and quiet. Many a night she would stand at the open window and gaze up through the dark-blue water where the fishes frisked with waving fins and tails. She could see the moon and stars; their light was rather pale, to be sure, but seen through the water they looked much larger than they do to us. If ever a kind of dark cloud glided along beneath them, she knew that it was either a whale swimming over her, or a ship full of human people. Those humans never imagined that a beautiful little mermaid was below, stretching up her white hands towards the keel.

And now came the time when the eldest princess was fifteen, and was allowed to rise to the surface. As soon as she was home again she had a hundred things to tell the others. But what did 5 she like best of all? Lying on a sandbank in the moonlight when the sea was calm, she told them, gazing at the big city, near to the coast, where the lights were twinkling like a hundred stars, listening to the busy noise and stir of traffic and people, seeing all the towers and spires of the churches, hearing the ringing of the bells. And just because she couldn't go to the city, she longed to do this more than anything.

Oh, how intently the youngest sister listened! And later in the evening, when she stood at the open window and gazed up through the dark-blue water, she thought of the great city, and then she seemed to hear the ring of church bells echoing all the way down to her.

The next year the second sister was allowed to rise up through the water and swim wherever she wished. She reached the surface just as the sun was going down, and that was the sight that she thought loveliest of all. The whole sky was a blaze of gold, she said; as for the clouds – well, she couldn't find words to describe how beautiful they were, crimson and violet, sailing high overhead. But moving much more swiftly, a flock of wild swans like a long white ribbon had flown across the waves towards the setting sun. She too had swum towards the sun, but it sank in the water, and the brightness vanished from sea and sky.

The year after that, the third sister had her chance. She was the most adventurous of the lot, and swam up a wide river that flowed into the sea. She saw green hills planted with grape-vines; she had glimpses of farms and castles through the trees of the great forests. She heard the singing of birds; she felt the warmth of the sun — indeed, it was so hot that she often had to dive down to cool her burning face. In the curve of a little bay a group of human children were splashing about in the water, quite naked; she wanted to play with them, but they scampered off in a fright.

The fourth sister was not so bold. She kept to mid-ocean, well away from the shore, and that, she declared, gave the best view of all; you could see for miles around. She had seen ships, but so far away that they looked like seagulls. The friendly dolphins had turned somersaults; great 7 whales had spouted jets of water – it was like being surrounded by a hundred waterfalls.

Then came the turn of the fifth sister. Her birthday happened to fall in winter, and so she saw what the others had not seen on their first view of the world above. The sea looked quite green; great icebergs floated about, each one as beautiful as a pearl, she said – yet vaster than the church towers built by men. They appeared in the strangest shapes, glittering like diamonds. She had seated herself on one of the largest, and the sailors in passing ships were filled with terror, and steered in wide curves as far away as they could get from the iceberg where she sat, her long hair streaming in the wind. Late that evening the sky had become heavy and overcast; lightning flashed; thunder rolled and rumbled, and the dark waves lifted huge blocks of ice high into the air. Sails were lowered on all the ships; humans aboard were struck with fear and dread; but the mermaid still sat peacefully on her floating iceberg, and calmly watched the violet flashes of lightning zigzagging down into the glittering sea.

The first time each of the sisters rose above the surface she was enchanted by all the new and wonderful sights; but now that the five were old enough to journey up whenever they liked, they soon lost interest; after a short time at the surface they longed to be home again. The most beautiful place in the world was deep beneath the sea.

Still, there were many evenings when the five sisters would link arms and rise to the surface together. They had lovely voices – no human voice was ever so hauntingly beautiful – and when a storm blew up, and they thought that a ship might be wrecked, they would swim in front of the vessel and sing about the delights of their world beneath the sea; the sailors should have no fear of coming there. But the sailors never understood the songs; they fancied they were hearing the sound of the storm. Nor could they ever see for themselves the paradise down below, for when the ship sank, they were drowned, and only drowned men ever reached the Mer-King's palace.

On those evenings, the youngest was left behind all alone, gazing after them. She would have cried, but a mermaid has no tears, and that makes her feel more grief than if she had.

And then at last she was fifteen.

'There now! We're getting you off our hands at last!' said her grandmother, the old queen Mother. 'Come along, and let me dress you up like your sisters.' And she put a wreath of white lilies on her head, but every petal was really half a pearl. 'Good-bye,' the little mermaid said, and floated up through the water as lightly as a bubble.

The sun had just set when her head touched the surface, but the clouds still had a gleam of gold and rose. Up in the pale pink sky the evening star shone out, clear and radiant; the air was soft and mild, and the sea was calm as glass. A great three-masted ship was lying there; only one sail was set, because there wasn't a breath of wind, and the sailors were idly waiting in the rigging and yard-arms. There were sounds of music and singing, and as the night grew darker hundreds of coloured lanterns lit the scene; it looked as if flags of all the nations were flying in the wind.

The little mermaid swam right up to a port-hole. Every time she rose with the lift of the waves she could see through the clear glass a crowd of people in splendid clothes – and the handsomest of all was a young prince with large dark eyes. He could not have been much older than sixteen – in fact, this was his birth-day, and the cause of all the excitement. Now sailors began to dance on the decks, and when the young prince stepped out among them, over a hundred rockets shot up in the air. They made the night as bright as day, so that the little mermaid was quite terrified, and dived down under the water. But she soon popped up her head again, and then she thought that all the stars of heaven were falling down to-wards her. She had never seen fireworks. Catherine-wheels were spinning round like suns; rockets like fiery fishes soared into the sky, and all this was reflected in the sea. On the ship itself there was so much light that you could make out the smallest rope, and the 11 features of every face. Oh, how handsome the young prince was! There he stood, shaking hands with one guest after another, laughing and smiling, while the music rang out into the night.

It was growing late, but the little mermaid could not take her eyes from the ship and the handsome prince. The coloured lamps were put out; no more rockets flew up; no more guns were fired. Yet deep down in the sea there was a murmuring and a rumbling. The waves rose higher; great clouds massed together; lightning flashed in the distance – a terrible storm was on the way. And so the crew took in sail as the great ship tossed about. The waves rose like huge black mountains, higher than the masts themselves; but the ship dived down like a swan between the billows and then rode up again on the towering crests. To the little mermaid all this was delightful – but it was no joke to the sailors. The vessel creaked and cracked; its thick planks bent under the pounding blows of the waves, the mast snapped in the middle – and then the ship heeled over on its side, and water came rushing into the hold. Now at last the little mermaid realized that they were in danger; even she herself had to look out for the broken beams and planks that were churning about in the water. At one moment it was so pitch black that she could see nothing at all; then, when lightning flashed, it was so bright that she could distinguish every one on board. They all seemed desperately trying to save their own lives; but she looked about only for one, the young prince. And just as the ship broke up she saw him, sinking down, drawn below into the deep heart of the sea.

For a moment she felt nothing but joy, for he would be coming into her own country; but then she remembered that humans could not live in the water, and that only as a drowned man could he ever enter her father's palace. No, he must not die! So she swam out through the drifting, jostling beams; they might have crushed her, but the thought never entered her head. Then, diving deep into the water, and rising up high with the waves, she at last reached the young prince, who could scarcely keep afloat any longer in the raging sea. His arms and legs were 13 almost too weak to move; his beautiful eyes were closed, and he would certainly have drowned if the little mermaid had not come. She held his head above the water and let the waves carry the two of them where they would.

When morning came, the storm was over, but not a trace of the ship was to be seen. The sun rose, flame-red and brilliant, out of the water, and seemed to bring a tinge of life to the pale face of the prince; but his eyes remained shut. The mermaid kissed his forehead and stroked back his wet hair. The thought came to her that he was very much like the marble statue in her own little garden; she kissed him again. Oh, if only he would live!

And now she saw dry land in front of her, and high blue mountains whose tops were white with snow. Not far from the shore were lovely green woods, and before them stood a church, or abbey – she did not know what to call it, but a building of that kind. Orange and lemon trees grew in its garden, and tall palms by the gate. Nearby the sea formed a little bay, very calm and 14 still, but deep, with cliffs all round where fine white sand had piled. She swam to this bay with the handsome prince, and laid him on the sand, in the warmth of the sun, taking care that his head lay well away from the sea.

Now the bells rang out in the great white building. So the little mermaid swam further out and hid behind some rocks rising out of the water, covering herself in sea foam so that no one would notice her. From there she watched to see who would come to rescue the poor prince lying in the sand. Quite soon a young girl appeared. The sight of the half-drowned figure seemed to frighten her, but only for a moment. Then she went and fetched other people, and the mermaid saw the prince revive and smile at everybody around him. But he did not turn and smile at her, for of course, he had no idea that she was the one who saved him. She felt terribly sad, and after he had been taken into the building she dived down sorrowfully into the water and returned to her father's palace.

She had always been quiet and thoughtful, but now she became much more so. Her sisters asked what she had seen on her first journey into the human world, but she told them nothing.

On many evenings, and many mornings, she glided up to the place where she had left the prince. She saw the fruit grow ripe in the garden, and she saw it gathered in; she saw the snow melt on the high mountains – but she never saw the prince. Her one comfort was to sit in her little garden clasping her arms round the beautiful marble statue which was so much like the prince. But she no longer tended her flowers; they grew like wild things, trailing over the paths, weaving their long stems and leaves in and out of the boughs of the trees until the whole place was in shadow.

At last she could bear it no longer, and told the story to one of her sisters; very soon the others knew it too – nobody else, of course, except one or two other mermaids who told only their best friends. One of these was able to tell her who the young prince was; and where his kingdom lay.

'Come, little sister,' said the other princesses. And then, with their arms over one another's shoulders, they rose to the surface and floated in a long row just in front of the prince's palace. It was built of a shining gold-coloured stone with great marble steps, some leading right down into the sea. Towering above the roof were magnificent golden domes, and between the pillars surrounding the building stood marble statues; they almost seemed alive. Through the glass of the tall windows you could see into splendid halls, hung with priceless silken curtains and tapestries. In the centre of the largest hall a great fountain was playing, the water leaping as high as the glass dome in the roof. The sun's rays shone through the dome, lighting the fountain and the lovely plants that grew in the great pool below.

Now that the little mermaid knew where he lived, she would rise to the surface and watch there, night after night. She would swim much closer to land than any of the others had ever dared; she even went right up the narrow canal under the marble balcony, which cast its long shadow over the water. There she would sit and gaze at the young prince, who believed that he was quite alone in the moonlight.

Often in the evenings she would see him

setting out in his splendid boat with its flying flags, while music played. She would peep out from between the green rushes, and people who saw a silvery flash thought only that it was a swan spreading its wings. Many a time, later in the night, when the fishermen waited out at sea with their fiery torches, she heard them saying so much that was good about the young prince; this always made her glad that she had saved his life when he lay almost dead on the waves. But he knew nothing at all about that.

She felt closer and closer to human people, and longed more and more to go up and join them. There was so much that she wished to know, but her sisters could not answer her questions. So she asked her old grandmother; *she* knew quite a few things about the upper world, as she very properly called the lands above the sea.

'If humans are not drowned, can they live for ever?' asked the little mermaid. 'Do they never die, as we do here in the sea?'

'Yes indeed,' said the old lady, 'they too have to die; and their lives are even shorter than ours.

We can live for three hundred years, but when our time comes to an end we are only foam on the water; we are like the green rushes. But humans have a soul which lives on after the body has turned to dust. It flies up through the sky to the shining stars. Just as we rise out of the sea and gaze at the human world, they rise up to unknown places which we shall never reach.'

'Why, I would give all my hundreds of years in exchange for being a human, even for just one day, if I then had the chance of a place in the heavenly world,' said the little mermaid, very sadly.

'You mustn't think such things!' said the old lady. 'We are much happier here, and much better off too than the folk up there.'

'But is there nothing I can do to get an immortal soul?' asked the little mermaid.

'No,' said the old lady. 'Only if a human being loved you so dearly that you were more to him than father or mother; only if he clung to you with all his heart and soul, letting the priest place his right hand in yours, promising to be true to you, here and in all eternity – then you too 19 would share the human destiny. But that can never happen. The very thing that is so beautiful here in the sea — I mean your mermaid's tail — they think quite ugly up there on earth. Their taste is so peculiar that they have to have two clumsy props called legs if they want to look elegant.'

That made the little mermaid sigh, and look sadly at her fish's tail.

'Let us be cheerful,' said the old lady. 'Let us make the best of the three hundred years of our life by leaping and dancing; it's a good long time after all. Then when it's over we can have our fill of sleep; it will be all the more welcome and agreeable. Tonight, we'll have a court ball.'

This was something far more splendid than any we see on earth. The walls and ceilings of the great ballroom were of crystal glass, thick, but perfectly clear. Several hundred enormous shells, rose-red and emerald-green, were set in rows on either side, each holding a bluish flame; these lit up the whole room and shone out through the walls, giving a sapphire glow to the sea outside.

20 Countless fishes, large and small, could be seen

swimming towards the glass, some with scales of glowing violet, others silver and gold.

Through the middle of the ballroom flowed a broad swift stream, and on it mermen and mermaids danced to a marvellous sound – the sound of their own singing. No humans have such beautiful voices – and the sweetest singer of all was the little mermaid. When she sang, the whole assembly clapped their hands; for a moment she felt a thrill of joy, for she knew that she had the most beautiful voice of all who live on earth or in the sea. But she could not forget the handsome prince; and could not forget that she had no immortal soul. And so she slipped out of her father's palace, and sat in her little garden, thinking her sad thoughts.

Suddenly, echoing down through the water, she heard the sound of horn-music. 'Ah, he must be sailing up there,' she mused, 'the one whom I love more than father and mother, the one who is never out of my thoughts. To win his love and to gain an immortal soul, I would dare anything! Yes – while my sisters are dancing in our father's palace I will call on the old sea witch. I have always been dreadfully afraid of her, but she may be able to tell me what to do.'

And so the little mermaid left her garden and set off for the roaring whirlpools, for the old enchantress lived just beyond. She had never taken that grim path before. No flowers grew there, no sea grass even. All she could see was bare grey sand stretching away from the whirlpool, where the water went swirling round as if huge and crazy millwheels were turning all the time, dragging everything caught in them down, down into unknown depths. To reach the sea witch's domain she had to go right through these raging waters, and after that there was no other way but over a long swampy stretch of bubbling mud; the witch called it her peat-bog. Behind this lay her house, deep in an eerie forest. The trees and bushes were of the polyp kind, half creature and half plant; they looked like hundred-headed snakes growing out of the earth. The branches were really long slimy arms with fingers like writhing worms; from joint to

joint they never stopped moving, and everything

they could touch they twined around and held in a lasting grip.

The little mermaid was terrified as she stood on the edge of this frightful forest. She almost turned back – but then she thought of the prince and the human soul, and plucked up courage. She tied her long flowing hair tightly round her head to keep it from the clutch of the polyp-fingers; then, folding her hands together, she darted along as a fish darts through the water, in and out of the hideous branches, which reached out their waving arms and fingers after her.

Now she came to a large slimy open space in the dreadful forest, where fat water-snakes were frisking about, showing their ugly yellow-white undersides; the sea witch called these her little pets. In the very middle a house had been built from the bones of shipwrecked humans, and here sat the witch herself.

'I know well enough why you are here,' said the witch. 'It's a foolish notion! However, you shall have your way, for it will bring you nothing but trouble, my pretty princess! You want to get rid of your fish's tail and have two stumps instead, like human beings; then, you hope, the young prince will fall in love with you, and you'll be able to marry him, and get an immortal soul into the bargain.' With that, the witch uttered such a loud and horrible laugh that the creatures coiling over her fell sprawling to the ground.

'You've come just in the nick of time,' said the witch. 'Tomorrow, after sunrise, I wouldn't be able to help for another year. Now I shall make a special potion for you; before the sun rises you must swim with it to the land, sit down and drink it up. Then your tail will divide in two and shrink into what those humans call a lovely pair of legs. But it'll hurt; it will be like a sharp sword going through you. Everyone will say that you are the loveliest child they have ever seen. You will glide along – ah, more gracefully than any dancer, but every step you take will be like treading on a sharp knife. If you are willing to suffer all this, then I will help you.'

'Yes, I am willing,' said the little mermaid. Her voice trembled, but she fixed her thoughts on the prince, and the chance to gain an immortal

soul.

'But remember,' said the witch, 'when once you've taken a human shape, you can never again be a mermaid. You can never go down through the water to your sisters, or to your father's palace! And if you fail to win the prince's love, so that he forgets both father and mother for your sake, and lets the priest join you together as man and wife, you won't get that immortal soul. On the first morning after he marries another, your heart will break, and you will turn into foam on the water.'

'I am willing,' said the little mermaid. She was now as pale as death.

'But I want my payment too,' said the witch, 'and it's not a small one either. You have the most exquisite voice of anyone here in the sea. You think that you'll be able to charm him with it, but you're going to give that voice to me. The price of my precious drink is the finest thing you possess. For I shall have to put some of my own blood into it, to make it as sharp as a two-edged sword.'

'But if you take my voice,' said the little mermaid, 'what shall I have left?'

'Your beauty,' said the witch, 'your grace in moving, your lovely, speaking eyes – with these you can easily catch a human heart. Well, have you lost your courage? Put out your little tongue; I'll cut it off as my payment, and you shall have the magic drink.'

'Well, if it must be so,' said the little mermaid, and the witch put her cauldron on the fire to prepare the potion. 'Cleanliness is a good thing,' she remarked, and she wiped out the cauldron with a knotted bunch of snakes. Then she scratched her breast and let some black blood drip down into the pot. The steam rose up in the weirdest shapes, enough to fill anyone with fear and dread. Every moment the witch cast some different item into the cauldron, and when it was really boiling it sounded like the weeping of a crocodile. At last the brew was ready – and it looked like the clearest water.

'There you are!' said the witch, and she cut off the little mermaid's tongue. Now she had no voice; she could neither sing nor speak.

'If those polyps catch hold of you when you are going back through the wood,' said the witch, 'just throw a drop of the potion on them. You'll see!' But the little mermaid had no need to do that, for the polyps drew back in fear when they saw the potion glittering in her hand like a star. So she came back without delay through the swamp, the forest, and the roaring whirlpool.

She could see her father's palace; the lights were out in the great ballroom – no doubt they were all asleep by now. Yet she dared not go and look, for she was dumb, and she was about to leave them for ever. She felt as if her heart would break with grief. She crept into the garden, took one flower from the flower-bed of each sister, threw a thousand kisses towards the palace, and rose up through the dark-blue sea.

The sun had not yet risen when she came in sight of the prince's palace and made her way up the splendid marble steps. The moon was shining bright and clear. The little mermaid drank the burning drink. A two-edged sword seemed to thrust itself through her delicate body; she fainted, and lay as though dead.

When the sun rose, shining across the sea, she woke, and the sharp pain returned, but there in front of her stood the young prince. His jet-black eyes were fixed on her so intently that she cast her own eyes down – and then she saw that the fish's tail was gone, and that she had instead the prettiest neat white legs that any girl could wish for. But she had no clothes, and so she wrapped herself in her long flowing hair. The prince asked who she was, and how she had come there, but she could only gaze back at him sweetly and sadly with her deep blue eyes, for of course she could not speak. Then he took her by the hand and led her into the palace. Every step she took made her feel as if she were treading on pointed swords, just as the witch had warned her – yet she endured it gladly. Holding the prince's hand, she trod the ground, light as air, and the prince and all who saw her marvelled at her graceful, gliding walk.

She was given rich dresses of finest silk and muslin. All agreed that she was the loveliest maiden in the palace. But she was dumb; she could neither sing nor speak. Beautiful slave girls in silk and gold came forward to sing for the prince and his royal parents. One of them sang more movingly than the rest, and the prince clapped his hands and smiled at her. This saddened the little mermaid, for she knew that her own lost voice was far more beautiful. She thought: 'If only he could know that I gave away my voice for ever, just to be near him.'

Next, the slave girls danced in graceful gliding motion to thrilling music, and then the little mermaid rose on to the tips of her toes, and floated across the floor, dancing as no one had ever yet danced. With every movement she seemed lovelier, and her eyes spoke more deeply to the heart than all the slave girls' singing.

The whole court was delighted, and the prince most of all; he called her his little foundling. So she went on dancing, though every time her foot touched the ground she seemed to be treading on sharp knives. The prince declared that she must never leave him, and she was given a place to sleep outside his door on a velvet cushion.

He had a boy's suit made for her so that she could go riding with him on horseback. They rode through the sweet-smelling woods, where the green boughs touched her shoulders, and the little birds twittered away in the fresh green leaves. She joined the prince when he climbed high mountains, and though her delicate feet were cut so that all could see, she only laughed, and kept at his side until they could see the clouds sailing beneath them like a flock of birds on the way to distant lands.

At night in the prince's palace, when the others were all asleep, she would go out to the wide marble steps and cool her burning feet in the cold sea water; and then she would think of those down below in the depths of the waves.

One night, her sisters rose to the surface, arm in arm, singing most mournfully as they swam across the water; she waved to them and they recognized her, and told her how unhappy she had made them all. After that, they used to visit her every night; once, in the far distance, she perceived her old grandmother, who hadn't been to the surface for years, together with the Merman-King himself, wearing his crown. They

both stretched out their hands towards her, but

they would not venture as near to land as her sisters.

As each day passed, the prince grew fonder and fonder of her. He loved her as one loves a dear good child; but the idea of making her his queen never entered his head. And yet, if she did not become his wife she would never gain an immortal soul, and on his wedding morning to another she would dissolve into foam on the sea.

'Do you not love me more than all the rest?' the little mermaid's eyes seemed to say when he took her in his arms and kissed her delicate forehead. 'Yes, of course, you are dearest of all to me,' said the prince, 'because you have the truest heart of all. Besides, you also remind me of a young girl I once saw, and doubt if I shall ever see again. I was on a ship that was wrecked, and the waves drove me to land near a sacred temple, which was tended by many young maidens. The youngest of them found me on the beach and saved my life. I saw her twice, no more, but she was the only one I could ever love in this world, and you are so like her that you almost take her place in my heart. But she belongs to the holy 31 temple, so it is my good fortune that you have been sent to me. We shall never part.'

'Ah, he doesn't know that I was the one who saved his life,' thought the little mermaid. 'He doesn't know that I carried him through the waves to the temple in the wood, that I waited in the foam to see if anyone would come to rescue him, and that I saw the beautiful maiden whom he loves more than me.' The mermaid sighed deeply – weep she could not. 'The maiden belongs to the holy temple' – those were his words. She will never come out into the world, so they will not meet again. I am here; I am with him; I see him every day. I will care for him, love him, give up my life for him!'

But now the rumour rose that the prince was to be married, to the lovely daughter of the neighbouring king, and because of this he was fitting out a splendid ship. 'The prince is supposed to be travelling forth to visit the next door kingdom,' people said. 'But it's really to call on the king's daughter.' The little mermaid shook her head and laughed; she knew the prince's mind better than anyone. 'I am obliged to make this journey,' he had said to her. 'I have to meet the charming princess – my mother and father insist on that – but they cannot force me to bring her home as my bride. I cannot love this stranger! She will not remind me of the fair maid of the temple, as you do. If I have to find a bride, my choice would be you, my dear dumb foundling with the speaking eyes.' And he kissed her rose-red mouth.

'You have no fear of the sea, my silent child!' he said, as they stood on the splendid ship that was to carry him to the lands of the neighbouring king. And he told her of storms and calm, of strange fish in the deep, and the marvels that divers had seen down there; she smiled at his accounts, for of course she knew more about the world beneath the waves than anyone.

In the moonlit night, when everyone but the helmsman at the wheel was asleep, she sat by the ship's rail, gazing into the calm water. She thought that she could make out her father's palace, with her old grandmother standing on the highest tower, in her silver crown, peering up through the racing tides at the vessel overhead. 33

Then her sisters came to the surface and looked at her with eyes full of sorrow, wringing their white hands. She waved to them and smiled, and wanted to tell them that all was going well and happily with her; but then one of the cabin boys drew near, and her sisters sank below.

Next morning the ship sailed into the harbour of the neighbouring king's fine city. All the church bells were ringing; trumpets blared from the tall towers, while soldiers stood on parade with flying flags and glinting bayonets. Every day was like a fête; no sooner was one ball or party over than another began – but the princess was not there. She was being brought up in a holy temple, they said, where she was learning the ways of wisdom that her royal role would need. At last, however, she arrived.

The little mermaid waited by, eager to see her beauty, and she had to admit that it would be hard to find a lovelier human girl. Her skin was so delicate and pure, and behind her long lashes smiled a pair of steadfast dark-blue eyes.

'It is you!' said the prince. 'You were the one who saved me when I lay almost dead on the shore!' And he held the blushing princess in his arms. 'Oh, I am overjoyed,' he said to the little mermaid. 'My dearest wish − more than I ever dared hope for − has come true. I know you will share in my happiness, because no one anywhere cares for me more than you.' The little mermaid kissed his head, though she felt that her heart would break. His wedding morning would bring her death, and turn her to a wisp of foam on the sea.

All the church bells rang out; heralds rode through the streets to proclaim the news. Sweet-smelling oils burned on every altar in precious silver lamps. The priests swung incense vessels; bride and bridegroom joined their hands and received the bishop's blessing. The little mermaid, in silk and gold, stood holding the bridal train, but her ears never heard the festive music, nor did her eyes see the holy ceremony. This was her last day alive in the world, and she thought of all that she had lost.

That evening the bride and bridegroom went aboard the ship. A royal tent of gold and purple had been set up on the main deck with silken 35 cushions and hangings, and there the bridal pair were to sleep in that calm cool pleasant night.

The sails filled out in the breeze, and the vessel flew swiftly and lightly over the shining sea.

As darkness fell, lanterns of every colour were lit, and on the deck the sailors danced merrily. The little mermaid remembered the first time she had come to the surface, and had gazed on just such a joyful scene. And now she too was joining in the dance, lightly gliding and swerving as a swallow does to avoid a pursuer. She could hear the admiring voices and applause, for never before had she danced so brilliantly. Sharp knives seemed to cut her delicate feet, yet she hardly felt them, so deep was the pain in her heart. She could not forget that this was the last night she would ever see the one for whom she had left her home and family, had given up her beautiful voice, and had day by day endured unending torment, of which he knew nothing at all. An eternal night awaited her.

At last, well after midnight, the merrymaking

drew to a close. The prince kissed his lovely bride, and they went to the royal tent.

The ship grew hushed and silent; only the helmsman was still awake at the wheel. The little mermaid leaned her white arms on the rail and looked eastwards for a sign of the dawn; the first ray of the sun, she knew, would mean her end. Suddenly, rising out of the sea, she saw her sisters. They were as ghastly pale as she, and their beautiful hair no longer streamed in the wind – it had been cut off.

'We gave our hair to the witch in return for help, for something that will save you from death when morning breaks. She has given us a knife. Look! See how sharp it is! Before the sun rises you must plunge it into the prince's heart; when his warm blood splashes your feet, they will grow together into a fish's tail and you will become a mermaid once again, just as you used to be. You will be able to join us in the depths below and live out all your three hundred years before you dissolve away into salt sea foam. Hurry! Either he or you must die before the first ray of sunrise! Our old grandmother is so full of 37 grief that her white hair has fallen out just as ours fell before the witch's scissors. Kill the prince and come back to us! Hurry! Do you see that red streak in the sky? In a few minutes the sun will rise and you will be no more.' With a strange deep sigh they sank beneath the waves.

The little mermaid drew back the purple curtain from the tent door where the prince and princess slept; she looked up at the sky where the red of dawn began to glow, looked at the sharp knife, and looked again at the prince. The knife quivered in her hand – then she flung it far out into the waves; they shone red where it fell, as though drops of blood were leaping out of the water. Once more she looked at the prince, through eyes half-glazed in death; then she threw herself from the ship into the sea, where she felt her body dissolving into foam.

And now the sun rose from the ocean, and on the foam its beams lay gentle and warm. The little mermaid had no feeling of death. She saw the bright sun, and also, floating above her, hundreds of lovely transparent creatures. Through them she could see the white sails of the ship and the rose-red clouds in the sky. Their voices were like music, but of so ethereal a kind that no human ear could hear it, just as no earthly eye could perceive them. Without wings they floated through the air, borne by their own lightness. And now the little mermaid saw that she had become like them, and was rising higher and higher above the waves.

'Where am I going?' said she, and her voice, too, sounded like those of the other beings, so ethereal that no earthly music could even echo its tune.

'To join with us, spirits of the air,' they answered. 'We do not need the love of a human being to become immortal. We fly to hot countries where the stifling breath of plague carries death to humans, and we bring them cool fresh breezes; we fill the air with scent of flowers that bring relief and healing. When we have tried to do all the good we can for three hundred years, we gain an immortal soul and eternal happiness. You, too, poor little mermaid, have striven with all your heart to do good; you have suffered and endured and have raised yourself into the higher world of the spirits of the air. Now, you too can gain an immortal soul for yourself.'

The little mermaid lifted her arms towards the heavenly sun. On the ship the bustle of waking life had started again. She saw the prince with his beautiful bride; they were searching for her, gazing sorrowfully into the moving waves. She smiled at the prince, and then, with the other children of the air, she soared up on to the rose-red cloud which floated in the sky.

'In this way, when three hundred years are passed, I shall rise into the kingdom of heaven.'

'Perhaps even sooner,' one of them whispered. 'Unseen, we glide into human homes where there are children, and whenever we find a good child, one who makes its parents happy and deserves their love, God shortens our time of trial. The child never knows when we fly through the room; if its goodness makes us smile with pleasure, a year is taken from the three hundred. But if we see a naughty, evil child, then we must weep tears of sorrow, and each tear adds one day more to our time of waiting.'

The Emperor's New Clothes

MANY years ago there lived an Emperor. He was so passionately fond of fine new clothes that he spent all his money and time on dressing up. He cared nothing for his army, nor for going to the theatre, nor for driving out in his carriage among the people – except as a chance for showing off his latest outfit. He had a different coat for every hour of the day; and at times when you'd be told of other monarchs, 'He's holding a council,' in *his* case the answer would be, 'The Emperor is in his dressing-room.'

Life was cheerful enough in the city where he lived. Strangers were always arriving, and one day a pair of shady characters turned up; they claimed to be weavers. But the cloth they wove (so they said) wasn't only exceptionally beautiful but had magical properties; even when made into clothes it was invisible to anyone who was either unfit for his job or particularly stupid. 'Excellent!' thought the Emperor. 'What a chance to discover which men in my kingdom aren't fit for the posts they hold – and which are the wise ones and the fools. Yes! that stuff must be woven and made into clothes at once!' And he gave the two rogues a large sum of money so that they could start.

So the rascally pair set up two looms and behaved as if they were working hard; but actually there was nothing on the machines at all. Before long they were demanding the finest silk and golden thread; these they crammed into their own pockets, and went on moving their arms at the empty looms until far into the night.

After a time, the Emperor thought, 'I really *would* like to know how they are getting on.' But when he recalled that no one who was stupid, or unfit for his work, could see the cloth, he felt rather awkward about going himself. It was not that he had any doubts about his own abilities, of course – yet he felt that it might be best to send someone else for a start. After all, everyone in the city knew the special powers of the cloth; everyone was longing to find out how foolish or incompetent his neighbours were.

'I know, I'll send my honest old minister to

the weavers,' he decided. 'He's the right man, as sensible as can be; and no one can complain about the way he does his job.'

So the good old minister went into the room where the two rogues were pretending to work at the looms. 'Heaven help us!' he thought, and his eyes opened wider and wider. 'I can't see anything.' But he kept his thoughts to himself.

The two swindlers begged him to step closer; did he not agree that the patterns were beautiful? the colours delightful? And they waved their hands at the empty looms. But though the poor old minister peered and stared, he still could see nothing, for the simple reason that nothing was there to see.

'Heavens!' he thought. 'Am I really stupid after all? That has never occurred to me — and it had better not occur to anyone else! Am I really unfit for my office? No — it will never do to say that I can't see any cloth.'

'Well, don't you admire it?' said one of the false weavers, still moving his hands. 'You haven't said a word!'

'Oh — it's charming, quite delightful,' said the 43

poor old minister, peering through his spectacles. 'The pattern – the colours – yes, I must tell the Emperor that I find them truly remarkable.'

'Well, that's very encouraging,' said the two weavers, and they pointed out the details of the pattern and the different colours worked into it. The old minister listened carefully so that he could repeat it all to the Emperor. And this he did.

The two impostors now asked for a further supply of money, silk and golden thread; they had to have it, they said, to finish the cloth. But everything that they were given went straight into their own pockets; not a stitch appeared on the looms. Yet they went on busily moving their hands at the empty machines.

Presently the Emperor sent another honest official to see how the weaving was going on, and if the stuff would soon be ready. The same thing happened to him as to the minister; he looked and looked, but as there was nothing there but the empty looms, nothing was all he saw.

'Isn't it lovely material?' said the cheats. And

they held out the imaginary stuff before him, pointing out the pattern which didn't exist.

'I don't believe that I'm stupid,' thought the official. 'I suppose I'm really not the right man for my job. Well, I should never have thought it! And nobody else had better think it, either.' So he made admiring noises about the cloth he could not see, and told the men that he was particularly pleased with the colours and design. 'Yes,' he reported to the Emperor, 'it's magnificent.'

The news of the remarkable stuff was soon all round the town. And now the Emperor made up his mind to see it while it was still on the looms. So, with a number of carefully chosen attendants – among them the two honest officials who had already been there – he went to the weaving room, where the rogues were performing their antics as busily as ever.

'What splendid cloth!' said the old minister. 'Observe the design, Your Majesty! Observe the colours!' said the worthy official. And they pointed to the empty looms, for they were sure that everyone else could see the material.

'This is terrible!' thought the Emperor. 'I can't see a thing! Am I stupid? Am I unfit to be Emperor? That is too frightful to think of.' 'Oh, it is charming, charming,' he said aloud. 'It has our highest approval.' He nodded in a satisfied way towards the empty looms; on no account must he admit that he saw nothing there at all.

And the courtiers with him stared there too, each one with secret alarm at seeing not a single thread. But aloud they echoed the Emperor's words: 'Charming, charming!' And they advised him to use the splendid cloth for the new set of royal robes he would wear for a great procession taking place in the near future. 'It is magnificent, so unusual . . .' Yes, you could hear such words all around. And the Emperor gave each of the impostors a knightly decoration to hang in his buttonhole, and the title of Imperial Court Official of the Loom.

All through the night before the procession day, the rogues pretended to work, with sixteen candles around them. Everyone could see how busy they were, trying to get the Emperor's outfit finished in time. They pretended to take the stuff from the looms; they cut away in the air with big tailor's scissors; they stitched and stitched with needles that had no thread; and at last they announced: 'The clothes are ready!'

The Emperor came with his noblest courtiers to look, and the two impostors held up their arms as if lifting something. 'Here are the trousers,' they said. 'Here is the jacket, here is the cloak' – and so on. 'They are as light as gossamer; you would think, from the feel, that you had nothing on at all – but that, of course, is the beauty of it.'

'Yes, indeed,' said all the attendants; but they could not see anything, for there was nothing there to see.

'If Your Imperial Majesty will graciously take off the clothes you are wearing, we shall have the honour of putting on the new ones here in front of the great mirror.'

The Emperor took off his clothes, and the rogues pretended to hand him the new set, one item at a time. They then put their arms around his waist, and appeared to be fastening his train, the final touch.

The Emperor turned about and twisted before the glass.

'How elegant it looks! What a perfect fit!' the courtiers murmured. 'What rich material! What splendid colours! Have you ever seen such magnificence?'

'Your Majesty,' said the Chief Master of Ceremonies, 'the canopy waits outside.' The canopy was to be borne over his head in the procession.

'Well,' said the Emperor, 'I am ready. It really is an excellent fit, don't you think?' And he turned himself round again once more in front of the mirror, as if taking a final look. The courtiers who were to carry the train stooped, as if to lift something from the floor, then raised their hands before them. They were not going to let people think that they saw nothing there.

So the Emperor walked in stately procession under the splendid canopy; and everyone in the streets or at the windows exclaimed, 'Doesn't the Emperor look magnificent! Those new clothes – aren't they marvellous! Just look at the train! The elegance of it!'

For nobody dared to admit that he couldn't

see any clothes; this would have meant that he was a fool or no good at his job. None of the Emperor's gorgeous outfits had ever been so much admired.

Then a child's puzzled voice was clearly heard. 'He's got nothing on!' 'These innocents! What ridiculous things they say!' said the child's father. But the whisper passed through the crowd: 'That child there says that the Emperor has nothing on; the Emperor has nothing on!'

And presently, everyone there was repeating, 'He's got nothing on!' At last, it seemed to the Emperor too that they must be right. But he thought to himself, 'I must not stop or it will spoil the procession.' So he marched on even more proudly than before, and the courtiers continued to carry a train that was not there at all.

The Steadfast Tin Soldier

THERE were once twenty-five tin soldiers, all of them brothers, for they had all been made from the same tin kitchen spoon. They shouldered arms and looked straight before them, very smart in their red and blue uniforms. 'Tin soldiers!' That was the very first thing that they heard in this world, when the lid of their box was taken off. A little boy had shouted this and clapped his hands; he had been given them as a birthday present, and now he set them out on the table. Each soldier was exactly like the next – except for one, which had only a single leg; he was the last to be moulded, and there was not quite enough tin left. Yet he stood just as well on his one leg as the others did on their two, and he is this story's hero.

On the table where they were placed there were many other toys, but the one which everyone noticed first was a paper castle. Through its little windows you could see right
into the rooms. In front of it, tiny trees were

arranged round a piece of mirror, which was meant to look like a lake. Swans made of wax seemed to float on its surface, and gaze at their white reflections. The whole scene was enchanting – and the prettiest thing of all was a girl who stood in the open doorway; she too was cut out of paper, but her gauzy skirt was of finest muslin; a narrow blue ribbon crossed her shoulder like a scarf, and was held by a shining sequin almost the size of her face. This charming little creature held both of her arms stretched out, for she was a dancer; indeed, one of her legs was raised so high in the air that the tin soldier could not see it at all; he thought that she had only one leg like himself.

'Now she would be just the right wife for me,' he thought. 'But she is so grand; she lives in a castle, and I have only a box – and there are five-and-twenty of us in that! There certainly isn't room for her. Still, I can try to make her acquaintance.' So he lay down full-length behind a snuff-box which was on the table; from there he could easily watch the little paper dancer, who continued to stand on one leg without losing her balance.

When evening came, all the other tin soldiers were put in their box, and the children went to bed. Now the toys began to have games of their own; they played at visiting, and schools, and battles, and going to parties. The tin soldiers rattled in their box, for they wanted to join in, but they couldn't get the lid off. The nutcrackers turned somersaults, and the slate pencil squeaked on the slate; there was such a din that the canary woke up and took part in the talk – what's more, he did it in verse. The only two who didn't move were the tin soldier and the little dancer; she continued to stand on the point of her toe, with her arms held out; he stood just as steadily on his single leg – and never once did he take his eyes from her.

Now the clock struck twelve. Crack! – the lid flew off the snuff-box and up popped a little black goblin. There was no snuff inside the box – it was a kind of trick, a jack-in-the-box.

'Tin soldier!' screeched the goblin. 'Keep your eyes to yourself!'

But the tin soldier pretended not to hear.

'All right, just you wait till tomorrow!' said the goblin.

When morning came and the children were up again, the tin soldier was placed on the window ledge. The goblin may have been responsible, or perhaps a draught blowing through – anyhow, the window suddenly swung open, and out fell the tin soldier, all the three storeys to the ground. It was a dreadful fall! His leg pointed upwards, his head was down, and he came to a halt with his bayonet stuck between the paving stones.

The servant-girl and the little boy went to search in the street, but although they were almost treading on the soldier they somehow failed to see him. If he had called out, 'Here I am!' they would have found him easily, but he didn't think it proper behaviour to cry out when he was in uniform.

Now it began to rain; the drops fell fast – it was a drenching shower. When it was over, a pair of urchins passed. 'Look!' said one of them. 'There's a tin soldier. Let's put him out to sea.'

So they made a boat out of newspaper and put 53

the tin soldier in the middle, and set it in the fast-flowing gutter at the edge of the street. Away he sped, and the two boys ran beside him clapping their hands. Goodness, what waves there were in that gutter-stream, what rolling tides! It had been a real downpour. The paper boat tossed up and down, sometimes whirling round and round, until the soldier felt quite giddy. But he remained as steadfast as ever, not moving a muscle, still looking straight in front of him, still shouldering arms.

All at once the boat entered a tunnel under the pavement. Oh, it was dark, quite as dark as it was in the box at home. 'Wherever am I going now?' the tin soldier wondered. 'Yes, it must be the goblin's doing. Ah! If only that young lady were here with me in the boat, I wouldn't care if it were twice as dark.'

Suddenly, from its home in the tunnel, out rushed a large water-rat. 'Have you a passport?' it demanded. 'No entry without a passport!'

But the tin soldier said never a word; he only gripped his musket more tightly than ever. The 54 boat rushed onwards, and behind it rushed the rat in fast pursuit. Ugh! How it ground its teeth, and yelled to the sticks and straws, 'Stop him! Stop him! He hasn't paid his toll! He hasn't shown his passport!'

There was no stopping the boat, though, for the stream ran stronger and stronger. The tin soldier could just see a bright glimpse of daylight far ahead where the end of the tunnel must be, but at the same time he heard a roaring noise which well might have frightened a bolder man. Just imagine! At the end of the tunnel the stream thundered down into a great canal. It was as dreadful for him as a plunge down a giant waterfall would be for us.

But how could he stop? Already he was close to the terrible edge. The boat raced on, and the poor tin soldier held himself as stiffly as he could – no one could say of him that he even blinked an eye.

Suddenly the little vessel whirled round three or four times, and filled with water right to the brim; what could it do but sink! The tin soldier stood in water up to his neck; deeper and deeper sank the boat, softer and softer grew the paper, until at last the water closed over the soldier's head. He thought of the lovely little dancer whom he would never see again, and in his ears rang the words of a song:

> 'Onward, onward, warrior brave!
> Fear not danger, nor the grave.'

Then the paper boat collapsed entirely. Out fell the tin soldier – and he was promptly swallowed up by a fish.

Oh, how dark it was in the fish's stomach! It was even worse than the tunnel, and very much more cramped. But the tin soldier's courage remained unchanged; there he lay, as steadfast as ever, his musket still at his shoulder. The fish swam wildly about, twisted and turned, and then became quite still. Something flashed through like a streak of lightning – then all around was cheerful daylight, and a voice cried out, 'The tin soldier!'

The fish had been caught, taken to market, sold and carried into the kitchen, where the
cook had cut it open with a large knife. Now she

picked up the soldier, holding him round his waist between her finger and thumb, and took him into the living room, so that all the family could see the remarkable character who had travelled about inside a fish. But the tin soldier was not at all proud. They stood him up on the table, and there – well, the world is full of wonders! – he saw that he was in the very same room where his adventures had started; there were the very same children; there were the very same toys; there was the fine paper castle with the graceful little dancer at the door. She was still poised on one leg, with the other raised high in the air. Ah, she was steadfast too. The tin soldier was deeply moved; he would have liked to weep tin tears, only that would not have been soldierly behaviour. He looked at her, and she looked at him, but not a word passed between them.

And then a strange thing happened. One of the small boys picked up the tin soldier and threw him into the stove. He had no reason for doing this; it must have been the snuff-box goblin's fault.

The tin soldier stood framed in a blaze of

light. The heat was intense, but whether this came from the fire or his burning love, he could not tell. His bright colours were now gone – but whether they had been washed away by his journey, or through his sorrow, none could say. He looked at the pretty little dancer, and she looked at him; he felt that he was melting away, but he still stood steadfast, shouldering arms. Suddenly the door flew open; a gust of air caught the little paper girl, and she flew like a sylph right into the stove, straight to the waiting tin soldier; there she flashed into flame and vanished.

The soldier presently melted down to a lump of tin, and the next day, when the maid raked out the ashes she found him – in the shape of a little tin heart. And the dancer? All that they found was her sequin, and that was as black as soot.

PENGUIN CHILDREN'S 60s

ALI BABA AND THE FORTY THIEVES • *Retold by N. J. Dawood*

THE AMAZING PIPPI LONGSTOCKING • *Astrid Lindgren*

ANNE AT GREEN GABLES • *L. M. Montgomery*

AT THE RIVER-GATES AND
OTHER SUPERNATURAL STORIES • *Philippa Pearce*

CLASSIC GHOST STORIES

CLASSIC NONSENSE VERSE

THE CLOCKWORK MOUSE • *Dick King-Smith*

DEAD MAN'S LANE • *Joan Aiken*

THE DRAGON ON THE ROOF • *Terry Jones*

FOUR GREAT GREEK MYTHS • *Roger Lancelyn Green*

THE GREAT MOUSE PLOT AND
OTHER TALES OF CHILDHOOD • *Roald Dahl*

THE GREAT TIME WARP ADVENTURE • *Jon Scieszka*

THE HOOLIGAN'S SHAMPOO • *Philip Ridley*

KEEP IT IN THE FAMILY • *Anne Fine*

KING ARTHUR'S COURT • *Roger Lancelyn Green*

THE LITTLE MERMAID AND
OTHER FAIRY TALES • *Hans Andersen (Translated by Naomi Lewis)*

LOST DOG AND OTHER STORIES • *Penelope Lively*

THE MIDNIGHT STORY • *Margaret Mahy*

MOOMINTROLLS AND FRIENDS • *Tove Jansson*

MRS PEPPERPOT TURNS DETECTIVE • *Alf Prøysen*

THE NIGHT TRAIN: STORIES IN PROSE AND VERSE • *Allan Ahlberg*

THE PIED PIPER OF HAMELIN AND OTHER CLASSIC STORIES IN VERSE

ROBIN HOOD AND HIS MERRY MEN • *Roger Lancelyn Green*

SHERLOCK HOLMES AND THE SPECKLED BAND • *Sir Arthur Conan Doyle*

SMACKING MY LIPS • *Michael Rosen*

TALES FROM ALICE IN WONDERLAND • *Lewis Carroll*

TALES FROM THE JUNGLE BOOK • *Rudyard Kipling*

THREE QUIRKY TAILS • *Paul Jennings*

TOM SAWYER'S PIRATE ADVENTURE • *Mark Twain*

TOM THUMB AND OTHER FAIRY TALES • *Jacob and Wilhelm Grimm*

Some other books available from Penguin in Puffin Classics

AESOP'S FABLES *Translated by S. A. Handford*
ALADDIN AND OTHER TALES FROM THE
ARABIAN NIGHTS *by N. J. Dawood*
ALICE'S ADVENTURES IN WONDERLAND *Lewis Carroll*
ENGLISH FAIRY TALES *Joseph Jacobs*
HANS ANDERSEN'S FAIRY TALES *Translated by*
Naomi Lewis
JUST SO STORIES *Rudyard Kipling*
PETER PAN *J. M. Barrie*
THE WIND IN THE WILLOWS *Kenneth Grahame*